Humphrey's Tiny Tales

My Pet Show PANIC!

Betty G. Birney worked at Disneyland and the Disney Studios, has written many children's television shows and is the author of over twenty-five books, including the bestselling *The World According to Humphrey*, which won the Richard and Judy Children's Book Club Award, *Friendship According to Humphrey*, *Trouble According to Humphrey*, *Surprises According to Humphrey*, *More Adventures According to Humphrey*, *Holidays According to Humphrey*, and *School According to Humphrey*. Her work has won many awards, including an Emmy and three Humanitas Prizes. She lives in America with her husband.

Humphrey's Tiny Tales

My Pet Show PANIC!

BETTY G. BIRNEY

Illustrated by Penny Dann

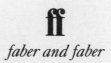

faber and faber

First published in 2011
by Faber and Faber Limited
Bloomsbury House,
74–77 Great Russell Street,
London
WC1B 3DA

Printed and bound by CPI Group (UK) Ltd, Croydon, CR0 4YY

A CIP record for this book
is available from the British Library

ISBN 978–0–571–24632–8

4 6 8 10 9 7 5

Welcome to
MY WORLD

Hi! I'm Humphrey. I'm lucky to be
the classroom hamster in Room 26
of Longfellow School. It's a big job
because I have to go home with a
different student each weekend and
try to help my friends. Luckily, my
cage has a lock-that-doesn't-lock,
so I can get out and have
BIG-BIG-BIG adventures!

I'd like you to meet some of my friends

Og

a frog, is the other classroom pet in Room 26. He makes a funny sound: BOING!

Mrs Brisbane

is our teacher. She really understands her students – even me!

Lower-Your-Voice-A.J.

has a loud voice and calls me Humphrey Dumpty.

Wait-For-The-Bell Garth

is A.J.'s best friend and a good friend of mine, too.

Speak-Up-Sayeh

is unsqueakably smart, but she's shy and doesn't like to speak in class.

Golden-Miranda

has golden hair, like I do. She also has a dog named Clem. Eeek!

Don't-Complain-Mandy

has a hamster named Winky!

Grandma Grace

is A.J.'s grandmother. She LOVES-LOVES-LOVES hats!

I think you'll like my other friends, too, such as *Repeat-It-Please-Richie, Pay-Attention-Art, Raise-Your-Hand-Heidi* and *Sit-Still-Seth.*

CONTENTS

I Go to the Pet Show

'Hang on, Humphrey,' A.J. said.

The car his mum was driving turned a corner and I slid across my cage.

'I'm trying!' I squeaked back.

Car rides aren't easy for hamsters like me.

I don't even have a seat belt.

I'm the classroom hamster in

1

Room 26 of
Longfellow School.

I get to ride in cars a lot because
I go home with a different student
each weekend.

'This is my lucky day,' A.J. told me.
'Mrs Brisbane picked me to bring
you home for the weekend. So I get
to take you to the Pet Show.'

A.J. and I had both been excited

when Mrs Brisbane told us about the
Pet Show.

'This is your lucky day, too,' A.J.
told me. 'You're going to win a prize!'

I crossed my paws and hoped he
was right.

'Remember, A.J., Humphrey might
not win,' A.J.'s mum said.

'There are lots of prizes,' A.J.
explained. 'He's sure to win one of
them. And I get to keep it!'

'Don't you have to share it with
the class?' A.J.'s mum asked.

'Humphrey's my pet,' A.J. said. 'At
least for the weekend.'

He pulled out a paper and read to
his mum while she drove.

'Here are the prizes,' he said,
reading the list out loud.

> *Most Friendly*
> *Best Trick*
> *Most Unusual*
> *Longest Tail*
> *Biggest Ears*
> *Loudest Voice*
> *Best in Show*

Just then my tummy jiggled and
joggled.

Was that because of the bumpy
road?

Or was it because I was worried
that I might not win a prize?

I didn't want to let down my friends in Room 26. After all, they were counting on me to win.

A.J.'s Grandma Grace leaned over and looked in my cage.

'He's one fine-looking hamster,' she said.

'Thanks a lot!' I said. But like most humans, I'm sure all she heard was 'SQUEAK-SQUEAK-SQUEAK.'

I liked Grandma Grace.

I liked Grandma's Grace's purple hat, too.

When the car stopped, I slid across the floor of my cage.

'We're here,' A.J.'s mum said.

'Yay!' A.J. shouted.

'Yay!' his younger brother Ty shouted.

'Yay!' his

younger sister DeeLee shouted.

'Goo!' his baby brother shouted.

'Eek!' I squeaked quietly.

*

The Pet Show was in a big building in the middle of the park.

Outside, it was nice and quiet.

Inside, it was NOISY-NOISY-NOISY. And what noises there were!

Barking, meowing, chirping, snarling!

Yipping, yapping, squealing, shouting!

Someone called out, 'Quiet, please!' But it still wasn't quiet.

'Here you go, Humphrey Dumpty,' A.J. said as he set my cage on a table.

I like it when A.J. calls me Humphrey Dumpty.

I call him Lower-Your-Voice-A.J.

because his voice is so loud. I have special names for all my friends in Room 26.

While A.J.'s family went to see the other pets, I looked around the room.

There was a lot to see, like dogs on leashes and cats in cages.

There was a lot to hear, like a screeching sound that made my whiskers wiggle and my tail twitch.

'BAWK!' a voice said. 'Crackers is pretty!'

I wondered what kind of creature was such a screecher.

Next, a soft voice said, 'Hi, A.J.'

I looked up and saw Sayeh from Room 26. I call her Speak-Up-

Sayeh because she is VERY-VERY-VERY quiet.

'Hi!' A.J.'s voice boomed.

Sayeh put a glass tank down next to me on the table.

'Og!' I squeaked.

I was unsqueakably happy to see my friend Og.

'Mrs Brisbane said I could bring him,' Sayeh said. 'I hope he wins a prize, too.'

'BOING!' Og said.

He makes a very funny sound. He can't help it. He's a frog.

He's also my neighbour back in Room 26. His tank, which is half water and half land, sits right next to my cage.

Next, A.J.'s best friend Garth showed up.

I call him Wait-For-The-Bell Garth because he's always the first one out of the door at the end of the day. He said he had come to see me win a prize.

'Okay,' A.J. said. 'But I'm the

one who keeps the prize because I
brought Humphrey.'

Another friend, Don't-Complain-
Mandy, arrived with her pet hamster,
Winky. Mandy's in Room 26, too.
She doesn't complain much since she
got Winky.

'I think Winky will
win Most Friendly,'
she said.

'I just hope one
of us
wins a prize,' Winky
squeaked to me from
his cage.

'Me, too,' I said.
Winky is one of my

13

friendliest friends, so I meant it. But I still didn't want to let A.J. down.

Richie showed up with a box with holes in the sides. Mrs Brisbane always asks him to repeat his answers in class, so I call him Repeat-It-Please-Richie.

'Hi, everybody!' he said. 'Want to see my new pet?'

'I do!' I squeaked.

A.J., Garth and Sayeh gathered round as Richie took the lid off the box.

'Meet Nick,' Richie said.

Garth's eyes opened wide. 'Wow!' he said.

'That's amazing!' A.J. said.

'Amazing,' Sayeh whispered.

What made Nick so amazing? All I
could see was a box.

Richie put the box down next to
me so that my cage was between the
box and Og's tank.

I climbed up my ladder to get a
better view, but all I could see were

some leaves and twigs.

Was Nick invisible? Or had he escaped?

'There's nothing there,' I squeaked down to Og.

'BOING-BOING!' Og sounded disappointed, too.

I was pretty sure that leaves and twigs couldn't win a prize at the Pet Show.

But I still wasn't sure I could win one, either.

The Show Begins

'The Pet Show is about to begin,' a voice said.

I looked up at the stage and was surprised to see Carl was speaking. Carl worked at Pet-O-Rama, the shop where I lived before I came to Room 26.

'Hi, Carl!' I squeaked.

He couldn't hear me over the

yipping, yapping, screeching and
snarling.

'Bawk! Crackers will win!' the
screecher said. 'Bawk!'

I was already pretty sure Crackers
would win the prize for Loudest
Voice.

Carl introduced the judges for the
Pet Show.

The first judge
was Ginger Jones.
She was a pet
groomer from
Pet-O-Rama.

She smiled and
waved to the
crowd.

The second judge
was Stormy Smith.
He was the weather
man from TV.

He smiled and
waved to the
crowd.

The third
judge was a real judge. A Justice of
the Peace.

Judge Lane
waved to the
crowd but he
didn't smile.

Then the
judges went to
look at the cats.

I heard a lot
of meowing,
growling
and hissing,
which was
unsqueakably scary
for a small hamster
like me!

Richie leaned down and spoke to Nick.

'Don't worry, Nick. You're sure to win,' he said.

Who was this Nick, anyway? Why was Richie so sure he would win?

'Og, maybe if I got up higher I could see him,' I said.

I scrambled to the top of my ladder, jumped onto my tree branch and climbed up to the very top.

Then I carefully got up on my tip-toes and grabbed the top bars of the cage.

Paw over paw, I worked my way to the corner. When I looked down, I felt a little dizzy, but maybe I would

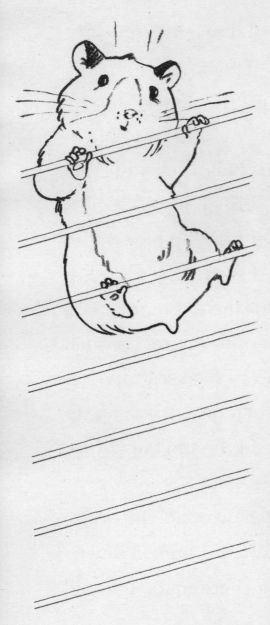

win the prize
for Best
Trick!

But after
all that
climbing, all
I saw was
that pile of
old leaves
and twigs in
the box next
to my cage.

Was
Richie
playing a
trick on the
judges?

'There's still nothing there, Og,' I squeaked to my friend.

Og splashed around in the water in his tank, but I knew he was disappointed.

'And now, the Parade of Pooches,' Carl announced.

The owners brought their dogs out to the centre of the room. Luckily, they were on leashes. I must admit, I've been a bit afraid of dogs ever since I came nose-to-nose with an unsqueakably rude one named Clem.

The dogs and their humans walked around in a circle while Carl introduced them.

One dog named Oscar was

LONG-LONG-LONG but his legs were SHORT-SHORT-SHORT. He looked like a giant hot dog. Carl said he was a dachshund.

Then there was a tall, spotted dog named Smoky, who held his head high. He walked when his human walked and stopped when his human stopped.

When his owner said, 'Heel,' Smoky followed right at her heels. Good dog!

Next came a teeny-tiny dog named Cha-Cha. She walked very

fast to keep up with her human.

Doodles was a shaggy
dog with no eyes at all.
At least I couldn't see
any under all that
fur. But he seemed
to know where
he was going.
Then my
heart went
THUMPITY-THUMP-THUMP.

I didn't need to hear Carl say the
next dog's name. I'd know that big
nose anywhere!

It was Miranda's dog, Clem. I love
Golden-Miranda. That's what I call
her, but her name is really Miranda

Golden. She is one of my favourite friends from Room 26.

I didn't love Clem. I'd met him when I spent a weekend at Miranda's house.

I still remembered his large, sharp teeth and his smelly doggy breath.

As Miranda led him around the

circle, the judges made notes.

'Next, the other pets,' Carl announced.

Other pets? Did that mean Og and me?

'Bawk! Crackers will win!' a voice screeched.

I hopped on my wheel and started spinning.

'The judges are coming, Og,' I told my friend. 'Be friendly, splash around, make some noise!'

I didn't hear a thing coming from his cage.

Why was Og so quiet? Didn't he want to win a prize? Did he want to let our friends down?

The judges walked towards the table.

'Remember, we're here to win, Og,' I squeaked. 'It's showtime!'

First, the judges looked at a creature called a bearded dragon. Eeek!

I thought dragons breathed fire and ate people. But this dragon

turned out to be a fancy lizard
named Lola.

'She's very unusual,' Stormy Smith
said.

'Very,' Ginger Jones agreed.

'Hmm,' Judge Lane said as he
made notes.

Then the judges looked at a guinea

pig, a turtle and a rabbit named Peter.

Next, they moved to my friend Winky's cage. Winky was born with one eye closed, so he always looked as if he was winking.

'Wow, he's friendly,' Ginger Jones said.

'Crackers is pretty! Crackers

will win,' that awful voice
screeched.

Now I could see Crackers,
sitting on her human's arm.
She was a huge bird with
green and yellow feathers.
And she was quite pretty.

'Ah, a parrot,' Judge Lane said, looking at Crackers.

Stormy Smith nodded. 'A fine-looking bird.'

The girl who owned her said, 'Sing, Crackers!'

The crowd all cheered when Crackers sang, 'La-la-la!'

I liked Crackers' singing.

I didn't like her large, sharp beak.

As the judges headed towards our end of the table, my tummy felt jumpy and jiggly again.

I heard Garth tell A.J., 'I know Humphrey's going to win a prize.'

'Of course he will,' A.J. said, but he sounded worried.

Maybe he wasn't really sure I could win.

To squeak the truth, neither was I.

Here Come
the Judges

First, the judges stopped at Og's tank.

'Show them what a great frog you, are, Og,' I told my friend. 'Do your very best.'

Everyone stared at Og.

Og stared back, but he didn't do anything else.

'BOING for them, Oggy!' I squeaked.

But Og didn't BOING. He didn't even splash.

He just stared at the judges. They stared back.

'Come on, Og,' Sayeh whispered. 'Show them what a good swimmer you are.'

Og kept on staring.

What did Og see? I looked out at the crowd.

I saw people, dogs, cats, dragons, birds and other strange creatures.

Maybe Og was scared.

'Don't be afraid, Og,' I said. 'Act friendly. Say hello!'

'BOING!' he said at last.

Stormy Smith looked surprised.
'What was that?' he asked.

'That's how he talks,' Garth
explained.

'BOING-BOING!' Og jumped up
and down.

The judges leaned in and looked interested until Crackers opened her beak and started squawking again.

'Crackers is the best!' she said.

Then Og stopped. He didn't make another sound.

But at least he'd tried. A little.

The judges moved on to my cage. Now it was all up to me.

'Who's this?' Stormy Smith asked.

'Humphrey,' A.J. said. 'He's a golden hamster.'

Unlike Og, I put on a great show.

First, I leaped up to the side of my cage, looked straight at the judges and squeaked hello.

'He's a friendly little fellow!'

Stormy Smith
exclaimed.

Next, I
hopped onto my
wheel and did a
fast spin.

'Look at him
go!' said Ginger
Jones.

I climbed
back up to the
top of my cage,
grabbed the
highest bar, and
swung there by
one paw.

Sometimes, I

amaze myself.

'Goodness,' Judge Lane said.

Next, I slid DOWN-DOWN-DOWN and dropped back onto the wheel. This time, I spun backwards!

My whiskers were wilting, but I kept on spinning as the judges made notes.

'Great job,' said Ginger Jones.

I was unsqueakably proud.

Then she noticed the box next to me.

'What's in there?' she asked.

'That's Nick,' Richie said. 'I'll make him move.'

The judges came closer as Richie poked around inside the box.

I stopped spinning so I could watch.

Even Judge Lane looked surprised. 'I thought it was a stick until it moved,' he said.

I thought I saw a stick move in there, too. But a stick doesn't move all by itself, does it?

'It's a stick insect,' Richie explained.

'That's why I call him Nick – Nick the Stick.'

People crowded round to see Nick.

'The stick is an insect!' I squeaked to Og.

'BOING-BOING!' Og twanged loudly.

He was probably excited because he likes insects.

He likes them for dinner. And breakfast, too. Yuck!

'BOING-BOING-BOING!' Og repeated.

People in the crowd chuckled.

'Og has a pretty loud voice,' A.J. said.

I guess he still hoped that Og could win a prize.

So did I.

Next, Carl asked the owners to bring pets with special tricks to the centre of the room.

Smoky, the spotted dog, rolled over and sat up and begged.

Cha-Cha, the tiny dog, stood on her hind legs and did a hula dance.

At least, that's what her owner called
it.

Oscar, the dachshund, sang. It was

more of a wail than singing.

Crackers tried to drown him out by singing 'La-la-la.'

It was NOISY-NOISY-NOISY.
But I was still wondering what
kind of animal a stick insect was.
Was it an insect or was it a stick?

Luckily, I have a secret lock-
that-doesn't-lock that allows me
to get in and out of my cage
without humans knowing.

So while everyone watched
the tricks, I jiggled the lock and
slipped out of my cage.

As the door swung open, I saw
Miranda lead Clem to the centre
of the room.

I didn't think Clem was clever

enough to do a trick, but it turned out he could chase his own tail. I was just glad he wasn't chasing me.

While everyone watched Clem, I tiptoed over to Nick's box. I couldn't see over the top, but there were air holes in the side of the box. I got up on my tip-toes and peeked inside.

What an unsqueakably strange
sight!

Nick still looked like a stick, but
now I saw that the stick had eyes!
And it moved ever so slowly.

'Eeek!' I squeaked.

I'm sure no one heard me, because
the crowd was cheering.

I looked over and saw that the
people were cheering for a cat.

'I never heard of a cat doing tricks,'
I heard A.J. tell Garth.

'Me neither,' Garth replied.

But this cat did a great trick. His
owner held up a big hoop and the
cat leaped right through it.

Then he turned round and leaped

through it again!

The trick was so amazing I forgot I
was out of my cage.

Then something happened that
made me forget about Nick the Stick.

I wasn't worried about winning a
prize any more.

I was only worried about staying
alive!

A Matter of
Life and Breath

When the dogs saw the performing
cat, they got excited. I'd never heard
so much barking, howling, yipping
and yapping in my life.

But Clem was more excited than
any of them.

'Down, boy!' Miranda yelled as
Clem tugged at his leash.

She tried to stop him, but he pulled

the leash right out of her hand
and rushed towards the cat.
As the cat jumped
through the hoop
again, Clem
jumped right
after him!

Then a
strange thing
happened. Clem
stopped chasing the
cat and he sniffed the
air. I'm not sure what
he smelled, but he headed

straight for me!

That's when I remembered I was out of my cage. And if Clem got to me before I got to my cage, I'd be in big trouble!

Og tried to warn me. 'BOING-BOING-BOING!'

But there wasn't much else he could do.

Just as I reached the cage, I saw Clem's big nose poke up over the edge of the table.

I saw his sharp, shiny teeth.

I smelled his horrible doggy breath.

'Bad dog!' Miranda shouted.

She was right. He was a BAD-BAD-BAD dog!

'Somebody, stop that
dog!' Carl shouted.

'Humphrey's out of the cage!'
A.J. bellowed.

'Grab him!' Garth yelled. 'Quick!'

Before anyone could grab me,
Clem pounced. His jaws opened
wide.

Eeek! I took a flying leap and landed on his long nose.

Clem's eyes crossed as he tried to look at me.

I jumped again and landed between his ears. Clem didn't like that, so he shook his head — hard. I hung on for dear life to a clump of his fur.

Just then, Og leaped up out of his tank, popping the plastic top right off. He landed next to me on top of Clem's head.

Clem seemed VERY-VERY-VERY confused. I don't think he'd ever had a hamster and a frog on his head before.

He lowered his head and shook it again to get us off.

Og and I slid straight down to the floor!

'Run, Og. Hurry!' I squeaked as I raced away from Clem.

My heart was pounding. As we ran and hopped, hopped and ran, there was panic at the Pet Show, but no one was more scared than I was.

'Bad dog! Come back!' That was Miranda.

'Bad-dog – bawk!' That was Crackers.

'Somebody, stop that dog!' That was Carl again.

I could smell Clem's awful doggy breath and knew he was close behind.

Then, everything went dark. The world turned upside down. Og and I were flipped up, down and all around.

'I've got them!' a voice called out.

'Eeek!' I squeaked.

Finally, I could see light again.

'A hat always comes in handy,' Grandma Grace said.

She was smiling down at us. I

didn't know who she was at first, because she wasn't wearing her purple hat.

Then I saw what had happened. Og and I were inside Grandma Grace's hat. She had thrown it over us, then scooped the hat up. That purple hat saved our lives.

'Thanks, Grandma Grace,' I
squeaked weakly.

'BOING!' Og sounded pretty tired,
too.

Lots of humans gathered round
to look at us, but Grandma Grace
shooed them away.

'Let these little fellows rest,' she said.

I liked Grandma Grace and her
purple hat VERY-VERY-VERY
much.

★

I was happy to be back in my cage
and to hear Og splashing in his tank.

Then the judges stepped forward
and said they had chosen the winners
of the prizes.

My tummy did a flip-flop. I
hoped my friends wouldn't be too
disappointed if I didn't win a prize.

'It was a tough choice,' Stormy
Smith said.

'We think you're all winners,'
Ginger Jones said.

'Let's hand out the rosettes,' Judge
Lane said.

I crossed my toes as they awarded
the prizes.

The Best Trick
prize went to the
cat who jumped
through the
hoop. His name
was Noodles.

Peter the
rabbit won the
Biggest Ears
prize. That was
no surprise!

The prize for
the Longest Tail went to Clem.

I suppose he did have the longest
tail, but I wouldn't have given him a

prize for anything. Still, I was happy for Miranda.

Crackers won the prize for the Loudest Voice.

'Crackers is the best!' the parrot squawked.

She was loud, all right. I just wished that sometimes she'd keep her beak shut.

'There were two winners for Most Unusual Pet,' Stormy Smith said.

My ears pricked up. Maybe Og could get a prize here.

But the two winners were Nick the Stick and Lola the bearded dragon.

Og had lost to a bearded lady and a stick!

I was happy for Richie, though. He
jumped up and down and high-fived
his friends.

'I'm sure you'll win the next prize,
Humphrey,' A.J. whispered to me.

I noticed that A.J. had his fingers
crossed, so I crossed my paws as well.

Stormy Smith announced another
prize with two winners.

'The prizes for Most Friendly Pet
go to Winky and Humphrey,' he said.
I could hardly believe my tiny ears.

'BOING-BOING!' Og twanged.
Everybody cheered and I was
HAPPY-HAPPY-HAPPY to share
the prize with Winky.

'I won!' A.J. shouted. 'I won a
prize!'

'No, Humphrey won,' Garth said.
'He's the class pet of everybody in
Room 26. Why should you get the
prize?'

A.J. looked surprised. 'Well, I
brought him here, didn't I?'

He leaned down next to my cage.
'Way to go, Humphrey,' he said.

But I thought that not sharing my
prize wasn't the way to go at all.

When Mandy and A.J. stepped up
to accept the prizes, A.J. asked if he
could say something.

Stormy Smith handed A.J. the
microphone. Not that A.J. needed
one with his loud voice.

'I want to share this prize with

everybody in Room 26,' he said.
'Humphrey's our classroom hamster.
He belongs to us all.'

I was unsqueakably proud of A.J.
for sharing!

The judges gave the prize for Best
in Show to Smoky, the spotted dog.

The crowd cheered and I joined in.

I thought all the prizes had been awarded, but the judges weren't finished.

'We are also giving a very special prize,' Stormy Smith said with a big smile on his face.

'Og the Frog gets the prize for Best Friend, for helping Humphrey.'

Og won a special prize for helping me!

Sayeh looked very proud and so did my other friends from Room 26. Stormy handed the microphone to her.

If there's one thing Sayeh doesn't like, it's speaking in front of other people. But in her soft voice, she also shared the prize with everyone in Room 26.

As the crowd clapped, my friends started chanting, 'Og, Og, Og, Og!'

No one squeaked louder than I did.

When things quietened down again, Stormy Smith said, 'We'd also like to thank Mrs Grace Cook,' he said. 'Thanks for your quick thinking and your purple hat.'

Grandma Grace waved to the cheering crowd.

My tiny paws were getting sore from clapping!

★

'THANKS-THANKS-THANKS for

helping me,' I told Og when the noise died down.

Og dived to the bottom of his tank.

Then he did three backwards somersaults.

It was a prize-winning trick, but no one saw it except me.

Home,
Sweet Home

On the way home, A.J. seemed quieter than usual.

'What's the matter?' asked Grandma Grace. 'You're not usually so quiet.

'I just wish I could get a pet,' he said. 'But Dad says not right now.'

I wished he could, too. He always took GOOD-GOOD-GOOD care of me.

'You already have a great pet,'
Grandma said. 'He's right here in the
car. And he's got a big, shiny rosette!'

A.J. sighed. 'But I have to share
Humphrey with everyone in Room
26.'

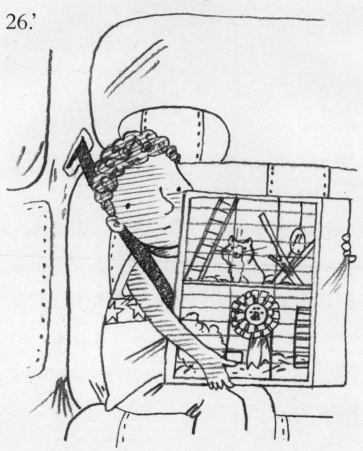

Grandma chuckled. 'You have to share me, too.'

It was true. A.J. had to share his grandma with his brothers and sister.

'But you know how much I love you,' Grandma said. 'I'll bet Humphrey feels the same way about you.'

Grandma Grace was one smart human.

'It's TRUE-TRUE-TRUE,' I squeaked.

A.J. laughed. 'Humphrey Dumpty, you're funny. I wouldn't want any pet but you. And Og, too.'

That made me feel even better than winning a prize at the Pet Show.

*

A.J. couldn't wait for us to go back to school on Monday so he could show my rosette to our teacher, Mrs Brisbane.

He was PROUD-PROUD-PROUD.

So was I.

Everybody wanted to tell Mrs
Brisbane about what had happened
at the Pet Show.

'It was so funny to see that purple
hat running across the floor with
Humphrey and Og
under it,' Garth said.

'It was wonderful,' Mandy said. 'Although it was terrible that Humphrey was in danger.'

When I heard the word 'danger', I let out a loud 'Eeek!'

'But it was wonderful that Og was so brave and helped him,' Mandy continued.

Miranda looked as if she was about to cry. 'Oh, I feel horrible,' she said. 'My dog could have hurt Humphrey, or worse!' she said. 'I'm so sorry.'

She looked so upset, I felt sorry for her, even if Clem was a truly awful dog.

By the way, doesn't Pet-O-Rama sell breath mints for dogs?

'I hope Humphrey stays in his cage from now on,' Mrs Brisbane said, looking at me. 'I don't want anything bad to happen to you.'

Mrs Brisbane is an unsqueakably smart human.

'Richie, maybe you can bring Nick the Stick in one day for

our biology lesson,' Mrs Brisbane
continued.

'Sure,' said Richie. 'Any time!'

At the end of the day, when all my
friends had gone to their homes, Og
and I were alone in ours – Room 26.

I looked at the shiny rosette
hanging on my cage.

I looked at the shiny rosette
hanging on Og's tank.

'I'm glad we won prizes, Og,' I told
him. 'We made our friends happy.'

Og splashed around in the water.

Then I continued. 'But I don't
really need a prize because being
a classroom pet is the BEST-BEST-
BEST job in the world!'

'BOING-BOING-BOING!' Og
twanged.

Even though I don't really
understand frog talk, I was pretty
sure that he agreed with me.

Turn over for more
fun with Humphrey . . .

Try some of the
puzzles from my
FUN-FUN-FUN activity
book . . .

Tasty Treats Wordsearch

Mmm, I have so many favourite foods that I love to snack on! My pal Aldo knows exactly what I like and always brings me a tasty little something. Yum! Can you find eight tasty hamster treats in this yummy, scrummy wordsearch? They might be up, down, across or diagonal.

APPLE • PEAR • CARROT • NUTS
SEEDS • CHEESE • RAISINS • BROCCOLI

S	E	L	P	P	A	C	P	B
T	R	A	U	A	H	U	N	R
E	O	S	E	E	D	S	T	A
E	C	B	E	F	C	E	P	I
A	P	S	L	B	A	C	K	S
S	E	G	I	R	R	E	U	I
T	A	U	H	A	R	I	E	N
B	R	O	C	C	O	L	I	S
C	E	M	A	S	T	U	N	W

School Wordsnake

I've really gotten to know the students in Room 26 well during my time at Longfellow School. I can even spell all their names! Can you find their names in this winding wordsnake?

Use a pencil to draw a continuous line through the names in the grid (in the same order as the list below). The line will snake up and down, backwards and forwards, but *never* diagonally.

SAYEH	SETH
HEIDI	GARTH
ART	MANDY
GAIL	PAUL
RICHIE	A.J.
MIRANDA	

S	A	Y	J	A
H	H	E	U	L
E	R	T	A	P
I	A	G	D	Y
D	I	A	N	A
R	L	I	H	M
I	I	E	T	R
C	H	M	G	A
A	R	I	H	T
N	D	A	S	E

Boat Bonanza

YO-HO-HO! I once took an unsqueakably dangerous voyage on a tall ship across Potter's Pond. It was a thrilling adventure! Here are six pictures of me in full sail. Can you spot one picture that is slightly different to all the rest?

c

d

e

f

For the answers, and for more puzzles, check out my activity book!

Here are some of my unsqueakably funny jokes!

Humphrey's Fabulous Food Jokes

I'm **LUCKY-LUCKY-LUCKY** that my friends in Room 26 give me my favourite treats, like yummy veggies and juicy fruits. These funny food jokes are making me hungry!

Q. Why were the strawberries upset?

A. They were in a jam.

Q. Why did the orange st

A. It was out of juice.

hee hee!

What sits in custard and complains?

A. Apple grumble.

Q. What do you call a burger that runs away?

A. Fast food.

Q. What kind of snack swings from tree to tree?

A. A chocolate chimp cookie.

Q. What's the difference between bogies and broccoli?

A. Kids won't eat broccoli.

Q. What's white, fluffy and beats its chest in a cake shop?

A. A meringue-utang.

Q. What's the biggest dessert in the world?

A. The Trifle Tower.

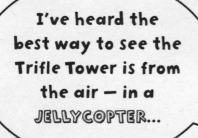

I've heard the best way to see the Trifle Tower is from the air — in a **JELLYCOPTER**...

Humphrey's Sleepytime Jokes

Like most hamsters I sometimes feel a little dozy during the day. In fact, maybe I'll have a little nap while you read these very sleepy jokes…

Q. Did you hear the joke about the bed?

A. It hasn't been made up yet.

Q. What do you call a sleeping dinosaur?

A. A dino-snore.

Q. What do you call a bull when it's asleep?

A. A bulldozer.

Q. Where do fish sleep?

A. In a river bed.

Q. Did King Arthur ever have bad dreams?

A. Yes, knightmares.

Q. What happens if you count sheep to help you get to sleep?

A. You have a baa-d night.

Q. How do you get a baby astronaut to sleep?

A. Rock-et.

Humphrey's Crazy Cats And Daffy Dogs

Dogs are **NOT** my favourite creatures – especially Miranda's great big hairy beast, Clem. Believe me, his sharp teeth are no laughing matter ... but these doggy jokes are!

Q. What's on special offer at Pet-o-Rama this week?

A. Buy a dog – get one flea!

Q. What happened when Clem went to a flea circus?

A. He stole the show.

Q. Why isn't Clem a good dancer?

A. Because he's got two left feet!

Q. What happens when it rains cats and dogs?

A. You might step into a poodle.

Q. What do you get if you take a really big dog out for a walk?

A. A Great Dane out.

ha ha!

For more jokes see my
ha-ha-ha joke book!

My next adventure coming in June 2011!

Humphrey and his friends have been hard at work making a brand new FUN-FUN-FUN website just for you!

Play Humphrey's exciting new game, share your pet pictures, find fun crafts and activities, read Humphrey's very own diary and discover all the latest news from your favourite furry friend at:

www.funwithhumphrey.com